LAURA CHEEVER

The Smith & The Spoons
A Fralsningdor Chronicles Short Story

First published by Cleavebond Publishing 2024

Copyright © 2024 by Laura Cheever

All rights reserved. No part of this publication may be reproduced, stored or transmitted in any form or by any means, electronic, mechanical, photocopying, recording, scanning, or otherwise without written permission from the publisher. It is illegal to copy this book, post it to a website, or distribute it by any other means without permission.

This novel is entirely a work of fiction. The names, characters and incidents portrayed in it are the work of the author's imagination. Any resemblance to actual persons, living or dead, events or localities is entirely coincidental.

Laura Cheever has no responsibility for the persistence or accuracy of URLs for external or third-party Internet Websites referred to in this publication and does not guarantee that any content on such Websites is, or will remain, accurate or appropriate.

First edition

This book was professionally typeset on Reedsy. Find out more at reedsy.com

A man's heart deviseth his way: but the LORD directeth his steps.

> Proverbs 16:9

Foreword

An introduction to gobbledygook, as spoken by the goblins of Fralsningdor:

- Fi'eren (fee-air-in) born of light
- Di'isha (dih-ish-ah) father
- Mi'isha (mih-ish-ah) mother
- Emph (emf) uncle
- Empha (emf-ah) aunt

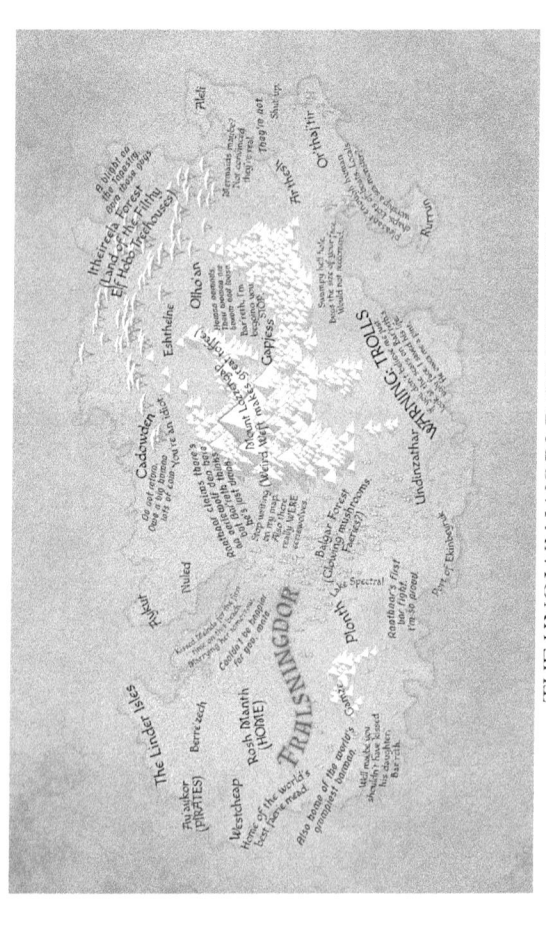

— THE KNOWN WORLD OF KORRETH —

As documented by Ranthnar La'arreth, crown prince of Fralsningdor. Circa 649 of the Second Epoch.

The Smith & The Spoons

— *Ten Years Ago* —

Fi'eren

"Fi'eren!" scolded Etta. "Look at your face! You absolutely can not deliver your first real order looking like *that*."

The plump, aged goblin woman bustled around the kitchen table, dabbing the corner of her apron in a jar of water as she came. Her dark green skin looked flushed from her fussing, and her silver hair, bound up in a knot, shone in the clear morning light as she walked.

"Empha," complained Fi'eren, olive green ears shifting to red as she scrubbed his soot stained face with her apron like he was a child.

Fi'eren may have been raised by Etta as if he were her own son, but he hadn't been a child in years. At twenty years old, Fi'eren was young for a full-fledged silversmith, as three years wasn't much time to train one's magic in such a dangerous craft. Hesh insisted that he was ready, though, and today he set out on his own as a real smith for the first time. Well… not entirely on his own. He'd made this set of silverware in Hesh's forge, and he'd continue to work there for the foreseeable future. But today was special nonetheless.

This commission, a set of charmed silverware for the local abbey, was the first order ever made out to Fi'eren personally, as opposed to his adopted uncle and master craftsman, Hesh Gor'rethnee. Fi'eren had spent nearly a month creating the set, slowly siphoning out his magic every morning into the molten metal until every last spoon, knife, and fork was charmed, forged, polished, and carefully packed into a neat, sawdust lined, pinewood box that he'd built specifically for the occasion. The box was sanded smooth but unoiled. It still smelled like freshly cut wood. He grudgingly shifted the heavy parcel under his arm to allow Etta better access to his face.

"Hush," said Etta, who was now standing on her tippy toes to reach Fi'eren's dirty forehead. Fi'eren sighed and leaned down so his adopted aunt could better clean off the ash leftover from the smoky forge. Fi'eren was shockingly tall for a goblin, and his last growth spurt three years ago had left him a sky scraping five feet tall. Which was conspicuously large in the all-goblin city of Plonth.

"Empha, it's just silverware," said Fi'eren. But he felt his cheek twitch with the vapor of a smile. He was both proud of his work and embarrassed by his aunt's theatrics. He'd come home to show her the completed set before delivering them and was beginning to have mixed feelings about the decision.

"It's silverware for the Looms, as you very well know," replied Etta tartly. Her lips quirked with a pursed smile, and her eyes gleamed with pride. "What's theirs is the Weavers, so really you've made these spoons for god himself."

Fi'eren grimaced. Etta's evaluation sounded grand, but he wasn't so sure he believed it. "The Weaver doesn't have a mouth," he quipped. "Invisible god and all that. How's he supposed to use the spoons?"

"Oh, quiet you," said Etta, fussing at Fi'eren's hair now. "You know what I meant. Now hustle on upstairs and change your shirt. The pants should be fine, but your sleeves are a mess."

"Empha," groaned Fi'eren again, standing to his full height now that Etta was satisfied with the presentability of his hair and face. "They don't care what I look like. They just want the silverware."

"Now," commanded his aunt, pointing at the stairway with an imperial finger. Both his age and his height still quailed under that stare, and Fi'eren leaned around Etta to place the box on the table so he could bound upstairs and change. He pressed a quick kiss to her silver hair as he drew back, and the older goblin woman beamed at him.

"You're a good boy, Fi'eren," she said, eyes growing misty. "And I am so proud of you."

* * *

An hour later, Fi'eren ducked past a lazy set of elven guards and stood at the front gate of the Plonthian abbey, feeling rather lost and strangely small. He'd been to the adjoining chapel for worship every First Day for the past nineteen years since he'd come to Plonth, but that gate was on the other side of the compound and was intended for public use. This gate was smaller and private, intended for the Looms themselves. He'd been told on the order form to deliver the silverware here for ease of access, which felt awkward, but Fi'eren could hardly argue with the request.

He could see the abbey gardens through the charmed silver bars. Goblin women in brightly colored dresses and woven headscarves bustled to and fro as they prepared the dark spring soil for fresh seeds and new life. Swallowing hard, Fi'eren shifted his grip on the pinewood box to better hold it under one arm, raised his other fist and knocked on the escutcheon. No one looked up from their work.

"Um... hello?" he called. "I have a delivery." He grimaced at the way that made him sound. Like a little messenger boy.

Luckily, one of the Looms seemed to have heard him that time, as she turned to the gate with pinched lips and narrowed eyes. Her dress was a rich shade of orange that matched her severe expression. Fi'eren resisted shuffling his feet. But only just. This was a place intended for women, holy women at that, and asking for entrance here at their private gate felt rather scandalous. The goblin woman set down a spade on the lip of a nearby wheelbarrow and marched over to the gate, hands on her narrow hips.

"What is it then?" she asked briskly.

"It's uh..." Fi'eren held up the unmarked box, and the woman raised a pale eyebrow. "Silverware," he finished lamely. "This is the order of silverware that was, uh... ordered. Last month?"

"Hmmm," said the woman, skeptically.

Fi'eren felt his palms begin to sweat against the smooth wood of his parcel. It was the first day of Jenuinth, was it not? He'd been told to come *today*... Right?

"Well, I guess you'd better come in then," she said sourly. Fi'eren let out a long, nervous breath as she opened the gate and gestured for him to come in. He smiled at her and nodded his thanks. "This way," she said, eyeing the large box under Fi'eren's arm. "Might as well carry it to the kitchens." Again, Fi'eren nodded his thanks.

They crossed the gardens and entered the abbey. Fi'eren avoided eye contact as well as he could, which was difficult as every goblin woman they passed seemed to be curious about the intruder. The journey was winding and Fi'eren was grateful to have a guide, even if she was a bit unpleasant.

"Here you are then," said the Orange Loom, in a tone that made it very clear that Fi'eren was an unbearable inconvenience. He wasn't sure he liked this "holy" woman very much.

Regardless, Fi'eren pasted on a polite smile that he hoped appeared convincing. "Thank you so much. Will you wait here or should I just…"

The woman turned and walked away.

"Show myself out," Fi'eren finished to her retreating back.

Frays and ashes. The trek to the kitchens had been an utter labyrinth of hallways. Fi'eren wasn't convinced he actually *could* show himself out. He might be stuck here, surrounded by these judging eyes forever. Perish the thought. Shaking his head, Fi'eren heaved a deep sigh, then rolled his shoulders down and back the way Hesh had always taught him.

A man can't look danger in the face if he's too busy staring at his own linty navel, Hesh always said.

Well, the small feminine Looms weren't a danger exactly, but Fi'eren did feel intimidated. He considered saying a quick prayer to the Weaver for courage, but discarded the idea. It felt foolish to pray over spoons, of all things. Good posture it was, then. He grit his teeth and marched firmly into the kitchens. He was going to deliver this order, gain a good reputation as a skilled craftsman, and become a successful smith here in Plonth just like Hesh.

There was a thump, a crash, a shriek, and the tinkling clatter of a hundred delicate knives, forks, and spoons scattering across the polished stone floor.

Burning Looms.

Fi'eren crouched down and began picking up silverware as quickly as he could, grimacing at the way sawdust now littered what had been an immaculately clean floor just a moment ago. He bit back a groan and felt his ears turning bright red.

Great loom above. He didn't think he'd ever been this humiliated in his entire life!

"Oh! Oh no. I am so so sorry! Here, let me help you. That was entirely my fault. I wasn't looking where I was going, and…" The pretty, chattering voice cut off as Fi'eren glanced up. He felt his jaw drop at what he beheld.

The girl crouching before him on the ground in the mess of sawdust and silverware was young. Probably close to his own age. She was dressed in a long-sleeved pink dress with a gray linen pinafore apron over the top. Not the clothing of a Loom. Her wavy brown hair was unbound and tumbled over her shoulders in a slightly unruly mess. Not the hair of a Loom either. Sage green skin flushed across her round, freckled cheeks with embarrassment, and she looked up at Fi'eren through long, dark lashes with a set of shockingly blue eyes.

"I'm so sorry," she repeated, and she wrinkled her nose self deprecatingly. Her nose was… utterly *bizarre*, truth be told. It was short and round and decidedly *pink*. The warm shade of her nose set off the vivid blue of her eyes and her eyes happily returned the favor. The young woman grimaced and kept talking while they worked. "Ka'ara always tells me to watch where I'm going. I supposed I will have learned my lesson this time… I hope." She sounded doubtful about that.

Fi'eren felt a chuckle bubble out between his lips, and the beautiful girl in front of him smiled shyly. She was lovely, friendly, *and* funny. Fi'eren wasn't sure he liked that. Or perhaps he liked it a little *too* much. She reached across his arm to grab the last stray spoon and Fi'eren felt heat prickle on his skin where she got close. Merciful Tapestry. He hoped he wasn't sweating.

Once all the silverware was packed back in the box, they stood, and yet again Fi'eren found himself surprised. This girl was *tall*. Just a few inches shorter than Fi'eren, which was still taller than most goblin men! Something about that made him... excited. This girl wasn't a waif who would blow away in a single gust of wind. This was a *woman* who could be held and not fall apart and...

Ashes, what was he thinking?! He didn't even *know* her!

"Don't worry about the floor," the girl said brightly. "I'll sweep up! Is this the new silverware Yeb ordered?"

"Uh... yes," said Fi'eren, feeling unbearably foolish. Why couldn't he think of anything clever to say? Something that would sound mysterious or impressive?

"I'm Fran," said the girl. "What's your name?"

What if he told a smithing joke? Hesh had a great one about a faerie and an anvil. But no. That might not make sense if she didn't know all the technical terms, and then he'd feel even more foolish. Wait. She'd just asked him a question. Did she ask why he was here? But he thought he'd just said that?

"Smith," said Fi'eren, desperately wanting this girl to know that he was the *craftsman*, and not just Hesh's messenger boy. Why did he even care? They'd only just met!

The girl smiled brightly and Fi'eren could feel his knees melting under the heat of that blazing grin. Her eyes crinkled at the corners when she smiled and her teeth moved just a bit to bite the smallest corner of her bottom lip. *Ashes*. Fi'eren wasn't going to make it out of this fraying abbey alive. This Fran creature was going to burn him to a crisp. What was *wrong* with him?!

"And do you have a first name to go with the last?" she asked, tucking a long strand of walnut hair behind her ear. It was a small ear. Less pointed than most goblins. Delicate in a way that made Fi'eren want to touch it *very* carefully.

"Fi'eren," he said. "Fi'eren Smith."

Oh no. Why did he say that?! He'd meant to explain that he thought she wanted to know why he was there, and that his name wasn't Smith but Gor'rethnee. Technically, it wasn't Gor'rethnee either, but that was the one he'd always borrowed from Hesh. It was too late now. He'd already made

10

far too much of a fool of himself.

"Well," said Fran. "It's a pleasure to meet you, Mr. Fi'eren Smith. I hope…" She flushed slightly and looked down at her feet for a moment before returning her gaze to his own. Fi'eren's stomach did a little somersault. "I hope I get to see you again." Her eyes flashed mischievously. "Soon."

"Oh you will," breathed Fi'eren. And he meant it.

For now that he'd met her, he couldn't imagine spending a single day out there in the bitter cold of the world without her blazing smile to warm him from the inside out. The magic in Fi'eren's bones purred at the thought, and he laughed a little. His laugh sounded awkward, but Fran beamed at him like he was smart and handsome and wonderful. Fi'eren melted even further.

Burning Looms. Fi'eren was a goner.

— *One-and-a-Half Years Later* —

Fran

Fran took a long, deep breath that shuddered slightly on the exhale. Her cashmere wedding gown was soft against her skin and loose in a way that left everything to the imagination. What lay underneath was for one set of eyes alone and for one set of *hands* alone. Fran's breath hitched with both nerves and anticipation at the thought. She glanced into the mirror above her dressing table and flushed with pleasure. She looked truly beautiful today. Even she could admit that.

The bright colors of her dress seemed to beam with joy, and the silver charms on her bridal headdress tinkled slightly when she moved. The traditional silver headband was woven into her hair with bright ribbons that fell down her back, along with her cascade of loosely curled brown hair.

It was tradition to pass down a cleavebond crown from mother to daughter for generations, but Fran didn't have a mother, so she hadn't had a crown. As such, Fi'eren had forged this headdress for her himself, and he'd carefully stamped their initials into the back of the first charm in the row. A secret love note that only she was aware of. He said he left the rest blank for their daughters and granddaughters and great granddaughters, and that he'd add their initials when it was their turn to bond.

Fran bounced on her toes with excitement, which set her headdress jingling again. Then she received a gentle hand to her shoulder that made her hold still.

"Now, now, dear," said Blue Loom Mella'a with a fond smile, "You'll see your handsome groom soon enough!"

"I know," laughed Fran. "I just…" She twisted her hands together before spreading them wide to indicate that she was lost for words.

The old goblin woman beamed at Fran with brown, tear-stained eyes. She pulled out a handkerchief and dabbed at both cheeks before folding it carefully and tucking it back into her pocket. "I know, love," said Mella'a. "I was the same way on my wedding day too. I practically *ran* down the aisle to meet my Kum'meph!" Her smile was both mischievous and melancholy.

Fran's brow wrinkled. "Do you miss him terribly?" she asked, thinking of Mella'a's husband who'd been killed by elves twenty years ago at the fall of Fralsningdor.

"Every minute of every day," said the old Blue Loom wistfully. "But I wouldn't change choosing him for the world, even after what happened. A cleavemate is a gift directly from the Weaver, Fran. We don't get to decide how long we keep them, but we do get to decide how well we love them while they're here. There will be days, weeks, months, or even *years* when loving Fi'eren is hard."

Fran's lips parted to protest. "Oh, I know that sounds impossible now, but trust me when I say it's true! That doesn't mean he isn't worth loving, though. Keep loving, dear. Keep fighting for your cleavebond. Keep trusting in the Weaver's plan even when your own plans fall apart! Today is your wedding, but tonight begins your *marriage*. There will be seasons of joy and seasons of pain, and many seasons of hard work and comfortable routine in between. Every day of it, no matter how hard, is a gift. And so is the man who walks those days beside you. Even his flaws are a blessing, sweet girl. For how could you ever learn unconditional love if your cleavemate met all the conditions?"

"Do you have any advice?" Fran asked quietly. "For loving him well?"

Fran had been raised in the Plonthian abbey by dozens of Looms who had been exasperating, but well intentioned and loving, nonetheless. She had more "mothers" than she knew what to do with, but today she felt the lack of her own true mother more harshly than she ever would have expected. The Blue Loom seemed to read her thoughts as she gently pressed a weathered hand against Fran's cheek. Fran nuzzled into the hand and felt tears prick at her eyes.

"Remember that Fi'eren is not a character in your story created to meet your needs," said the old goblin woman. "He's his own man. And you are both characters in the Weaver's story, the Weaver's Tapestry. You are both created to bring *him* glory. The fact that you can now do that together is a beautiful thing. Also..." Her eyes twinkled. "A goblin man is only as strong as his stomach, dear." The old goblin winked. "And your best weapon is a hearty meal."

Fran laughed and threw her arms around Mella'a's neck, squeezing her tightly and breathing deeply of the goat milk soap that the Looms used to wash their clothing. It was the smell of home, and Fran tried hard to etch it into her memory before she set off for a new adventure. A new family. A new home. "Then I guess it's good you taught me how to bake," she said with a sniff and a watery laugh.

"Yes, I suppose it is," said Mella'a, kissing Fran's hair. "Now come, dear. It's time. You have a wedding to get to and a husband to love."

* * *

"...through sickness or strife, famine or foe — I will offer my life for yours until the Tapestry frays or the Weaver calls us home." Fi'eren's voice as he spoke his vows was rich and warm and sounded strong enough to catch Fran, no matter how far she fell. And she *was* falling. Hard. All over again. She wasn't sure how she could possibly love him more than she did in that moment.

The final thread of the cleavebonding ceremony was carefully tied around their clasped left hands. They had each spoken a vow for every thread, and there were eight threads in total — red, orange, yellow, green, blue, indigo, violet, and finally gold. Gold for the light of the Weaver and for the gift of the and'drah.

Fran peeked up at Fi'eren and felt her heart trying to beat its way out of her rib cage. Fi'eren looked handsome and glowy in the candlelight of the chapel and through the dewy sheen of tears in Fran's eyes. His auburn hair was unusually neat today, carefully trimmed and styled. Fran smiled at the amount of effort he must have spent to avoid running his hands through his hair out of nervous habit. His wedding tunic was woven of bright wool threads and was tailored to a sharp cut that accented his strong silversmith arms. His long, crooked nose twitched a bit as he sniffed back a few of his own unshed tears.

"Does the Di'isha of the groom have the cuffs?" asked the officiant.

"I do," said Hesh, who stepped forward and opened a small wooden box.

Nestled there within the box on a tiny cushion of black velvet were two beautiful cleavebond cuffs. Fran gasped slightly, then looked back at Fi'eren with a grin. His returning smile brought dimples to his freckled cheeks. The cuffs were stunning work, and he knew it. He had insisted on keeping them a secret until the bonding ceremony, and this was the first time she was seeing them. Fi'eren's cuff was wide and sturdy, etched with simple designs — The cleavebond cuff of a working man. Fran's, on the other hand, was delicate and intricate. Patterns of incredibly realistic leaves wound up and down both the outside *and* the inside of the cuff. Even the parts that would never be seen had clearly been crafted with care. Fran had never seen a wedding cuff that was its equal. She'd been exasperated before with his secrets, but now she was glad he'd made her wait. With their left hands still clasped, Fran and Fi'eren took turns sliding the cuffs onto each other's right wrists.

Then it was time. The magical bonding.

Fran took a deep breath and cocked one eyebrow at Fi'eren as if to ask, "Are you sure?"

She knew he wanted to marry her, of course, but this next step of a traditional goblin wedding ceremony was expected to be difficult for him. Fran had magic in her bones but no way to cast it, which meant that performing the cleavebond ceremony would fall entirely on Fi'eren's shoulders. They were quite capable shoulders, as he had more magic than most goblins, but Fran had never before heard of someone forming a bond with a non-magical partner. The fact that he had even offered to try was incredibly sweet.

Fi'eren silently mouthed his answer as the officiant droned on, but Fran caught his meaning loud and clear. "Yes. Since the day we met, and until the day we die."

Fi'eren spoke his next vow out loud, the traditional words from the Pattern, and Fran felt her eyes grow wide as his magic flooded into her new, beautiful silver bracer. The magic felt like *him*. Like his presence at her side while they laid in a meadow under the stars. Like the timbre of his voice when he whispered that he loved her. Like the warmth of his hands as they pulled her close…

The officiant removed the cleaving threads and suddenly Fi'eren's hands were holding her for real.

"I now pronounce you cleaved to the glory of the Weaver. You may…"

But Fi'eren didn't wait for permission. His soft lips crashed into Fran's with a heady warmth that melted her down to the tips of her toes. He cradled the back of her head in one hand and tilted her chin back to deepen the kiss. His other arm wrapped tightly around Fran's waist, and suddenly she was in the air! Swept into his one armed grasp as he span her around and kissed her urgently.

Hesh whooped with joy, Etta and Mella'a cooed,

and the rest of the Looms in the abbey either sat silently with dour looks or else wept openly with disappointment.

But Fran didn't notice. She was too busy gasping with delight as Fi'eren took his hand from her head and hitched it under her knees, pulling into a bridal style carry and settling her more firmly into his strong, safe arms.

"Mrs. Smith?" he asked, with a mischievous twinkle in his eye. "I do believe we have an appointment."

"Fi'eren!" she replied, laughing at his audacious behavior. A blush crept up her neck and she tried to stifle the smile that pulled on her lips. He was her *husband*! She could hardly believe it. Fran leaned forward to press a kiss onto Fi'eren's cheek. Her *husband's* cheek. He turned his head at the last second, though, and caught her on the lips. This kiss was slower. Deeper. And it wakened something in Fran's middle that left her itching to leave the chapel and be alone with her new cleavemate.

Fi'eren seemed to be thinking the same thing, for he pulled back and nodded warmly to the only three people who were actually happy to see them wed. They clapped enthusiastically as he swept back down the aisle with Fran in his arms. He didn't pause to receive any half-hearted congratulations or snarky comments from the gathered Looms. At the end of the aisle, he kicked open the doors with one polished black boot, earning some self righteous gasps from the colorful assembly.

Then he strolled out into the glowing golden midsummer evening to take his new wife home.

Read the rest of Fran & Fi'eren's story in

— THE FRALSNINGDOR CHRONICLES —
by LAURA CHEEVER

About the Author

Laura Cheever lives in rural Wyoming with her husband, Andrew, and their four children, the legendary makers of mischief and shenanigans. When she's not writing or daydreaming about new stories, she homeschools the kids, reads a mildly-concerning number of fantasy novels, paints, plays board games, bakes mediocre sourdough bread, and plays old-timey hymns on the piano.

She hopes this tale has brought you light and hope, and urges all who seek the True Light and the Living Hope to read the greatest love story ever told, beginning with the Gospel of John, which can be read for free at www.esv.org/John.

You can connect with me on:
- https://lauracheever-shop.fourthwall.com
- https://www.facebook.com/lauracheeverauthor
- https://www.instagram.com/lauracheeverauthor

Subscribe to my newsletter:
- https://lauracheeverauthor.ck.page/profile

www.ingramcontent.com/pod-product-compliance
Ingram Content Group UK Ltd.
Pitfield, Milton Keynes, MK11 3LW, UK
UKHW030806170325
456354UK00002B/185